# Melting the Ice Between Us

--·--

## J.M. Jackie

# Disclaimer

This work of fiction is a product of the author's imagination and is not based on real events, individuals, or organizations. Any resemblance to actual events or persons, living or deceased, is purely coincidental.

The views and opinions expressed within this book are those of the fictional characters and do not reflect the beliefs or values of the author. The author does not endorse or condone any of the actions, behaviors, or ideologies depicted in this work.

Readers are encouraged to approach this book with an open mind and a critical perspective. It is important to remember that the events portrayed are entirely fictional and should not be taken as representative of reality.

This book may contain mature themes, including but not limited to violence, adult language, and explicit content. Reader discretion is advised, and this book is intended for adult audiences.

The author is committed to respecting the rights and privacy of all individuals and organizations. Any unintentional use of copyrighted material is purely coincidental and will be rectified upon notification.

Thank you for choosing to read this work of fiction. Your support is greatly appreciated, and the author hopes you enjoy the story.

# CONTENTS

# 1

## FROZEN FLAMES OF MEMORY

I have a gift, you see. A real knack for seeing homophobic assholes through a telescopic lens. Don't ask me how I got this gift. It was one of those strange quirks life decided to bestow upon me. Maybe it was the universe's way of compensating for the trauma. It's quite handy, though, when you can spot prejudice and bigotry from a mile away. *It's almost like a sixth sense.*

I stand by the window of my penthouse apartment, the city's twinkling lights stretching out before me like stars fallen to Earth. In my hand, I hold a crystal tumbler, the golden liquid inside catching the warm glow of the cityscape. It's the good stuff, the kind that burns just right. My phone incessantly buzzes on the coffee table. Rachel is probably going Hulk-smash over her keyboard.

The invitation to the high school reunion lies there too, a pristine envelope that contrasts starkly with the rustic surface of my coffee table. Willowdale Senior High. Just the name sends shivers down my spine. It was a nightmare factory, a place where adolescent cruelties were perfected. Yet, there's a strange allure this time around. A curiosity, a need to confront the demons I thought I had left behind.

"Good riddance too," I mutter, then I take a sip of the whisky, the liquid's warmth spreading through my chest. The reunion invite is adorned with names, and there it is as if taunting me from the page—Blake Bryan. The memories rush back, a whirlwind of emotions I've carefully locked away. Blake, the love of my life, or so I thought. Until he decided to rip my heart out and parade it in front of his jock asshat friends. The locker room incident is etched into my mind like a scar. A reminder of betrayal and humiliation.

*I've changed since those days.* At least the alcohol makes me think so.

The scars have healed, but they've left behind a different kind of strength. As I gaze at Blake's name on the list, I can feel a storm brewing within me. It's not just the past that's calling; it's the need to set things right. To face him, to show him that I'm not the same person he could walk all over back then.

I take another sip, the whisky's warmth mingling with the fire of determination in my chest. This time, things will be different. This time, I won't be the one who's left wounded. The invitation is a silent challenge. And as the city's lights continue to dance outside my window, I make a decision. The nightmare won't haunt me forever. Now is the time to step back into the fray and rewrite the ending I never got. *Blake Bryan, you're in for a surprise.*

My walking wet dream, and the source of my greatest heartache. Blake was my first for everything. But he was also the leader of the hockey team, stuck in his image and what people expected from him. He couldn't tell his parents about himself, so he let go of me. It's honestly sad how fear and the need to fit in can squash love.

I take another gulp of my drink, the amber liquid doing a delightful tango on my taste buds, while I casually ogle my chic penthouse apartment. It's perched on the ninth floor, like a bird's nest for the elite, boasting enough chrome, ceramic, and steel to make any minimalist's heart flutter. The walls remain bare, a deliberate choice to keep memories at bay. There are only a few pictures of close friends—those who stuck around when the world turned its back on me.

My phone buzzes again, and I pick it up to see Rachel Swan's name flashing on the display.

"Sup, ho?"

Her rich laughter is like a comfort that transcends time. "You heartless bitch, I called like ten times."

Checking my screen, I realized she had. "Oops, I meant to block you. My mistake."

"Shut up, Drama Queen," Rachel retorts, her voice teeming with playful sarcasm. "Ignoring my calls and texts? Did you finally get caught up in a torrid affair with a celebrity chef?"

"If you ever mention that show again, I'll slap you," I chuckle, rolling my eyes even though she can't see me.

"Then why, pray tell, were you ignoring me? Got some hot guy in your apartment?"

"If I did, I certainly wouldn't be talking to you," I quip. "No. It's just me and my right hand tonight. Sorry to disappoint you, but my love life is about as exciting as a potato exploding in the microwave."

Rachel's laugh fills my ear again. "True that. So, what's with the radio silence? I thought you'd be thrilled about the reunion, considering all the juicy drama it promises."

I sigh, leaning against the window frame. "Oh, I'm thrilled, all right. About as thrilled as I'd be to wrestle an alligator in a swamp. You know how much I loved Willowdale Senior High."

There's a pause on the other end, and I can practically picture Rachel rolling her eyes. "Kieran, you can't hide from your past forever. Plus, I've heard they're providing free therapy sessions this time. So, you're pretty much hitting the jackpot."

I smirk, shaking my head. "Well, that's definitely tempting. But I swear, if I see one person from my past doing yoga and talking about 'finding their inner peace,' I might just lose it."

"Fair enough. But come on, Kieran. This might be your chance for closure. Or at least a chance to flash your impressive pet food taster credentials."

I can't help but laugh this time. "Oh, you know it. I'm thinking of walking in there with a tiara made of kibble."

"That's the spirit," Rachel replies with a chuckle. "Now, promise me you'll at least consider going. I'll be your wing woman, and we can make fun of everyone together."

I pause, looking out at the city lights once more. *Well...insulting people is my area of expertise.* "Alright, alright, I'll go. But only because you promised to be my partner in crime. And if someone starts spouting New Age nonsense at me, I'm blaming you."

"Deal, Drama Queen. Now, hurry up and pack your tiara. We've got a reunion to conquer."

As we say our goodbyes, I can't help but smile. Rachel has a way of making even the most dreaded events sound like a grand adventure. With her by my side, facing the past doesn't seem so daunting after all. I am struggling to shake the feeling that this reunion might just be the chance to rewrite my story—one hilarious, sarcastic comment at a time.

***

THE FLIGHT IS AWFUL, to say the least. Screaming children dressed like adults; battling over overhead compartments and personal space. The baggage claim carousel spins like a twisted merry-go-round of chaos. The whole experience is enough to give me PTSD. As I step off the plane in Willowdale, Michigan, I can't help but wish I was anywhere else in the universe.

Rachel is waiting for me at the airport, bundled up in a coat that seems ready to wage war against the biting December winds. Her long dreads dance in the gusts, and her big, soulful brown eyes lock onto mine as if she's been counting the seconds until my arrival.

"Kieran! Oh my God, you're here! Did the flight suck as much as expected? Why do I even ask? It's always a circus. You look thinner. Have you been eating enough? Wait, don't answer that. We're going to the bakery first. I baked your favorites, and you can stuff your face while I fill you in on everything you missed in this godforsaken town."

I laugh as she drags me into a hug. Rachel's dreadlocks are meticulously styled into a crown, some locks falling just below her shoulders, causing several people to turn and stare. She's stunning and her voluptuous figure is enough to give Beyonce a run for her money. "I'm fine, motormouth. God, don't you need to breathe? How can you talk so much?"

"It's a gift."

Rachel has always been a whirlwind of energy, and it seems like she's only grown more enthusiastic over the years. I step forward, embracing her in a warm hug. "Rach, you're going to give me whiplash with that rapid-fire interrogation. And yes, the flight was a special kind of torture. But I'm here, alive and slightly traumatized."

"Alive is the important part. Traumatized is optional. But hey, let's turn that trauma into some sugar-infused joy. You remember my bakery, right?"

"How could I forget?" I reply with a smirk. "I'd recognize the scent of your cinnamon rolls anywhere."

She playfully swats my arm. "Oh, stop buttering me up, Drama Queen. Now let's get going. You need some serious comfort food, and I've got a pastry display that'll make your heart sing."

"Now you're speaking my language."

We make our way to her bakery, the familiar scent of freshly baked goods enveloping us as we step inside. The warm ambiance is a stark contrast to the frosty chill outside. Rachel leads me to a cozy corner table, laden with a mouthwatering assortment of pastries and treats. The air is heavy with the rich scent of brewed coffee and macaroons. The sleek pink interior is adorned with an array of confections, from pumpkin spice cupcakes to muffins that Rachel swears are "cream cheese orgasm-inducing." It's a sensory overload in the best way possible.

We settle into a corner, the comfortable atmosphere enveloping us like a warm embrace. As I take a bite of a decadent blueberry scone, she finally takes a moment to catch her breath. "Okay, now that your mouth is too full to fire off sarcastic remarks, let's get you up to speed. Remember Mark, the guy who used to have a crush on you back in high school?"

I nod, my cheeks puffy with a muffin, trying to suppress a grin as I savor the explosion of flavors. Rachel's dark skin glows like the sun-kissed earth, with a few dreads framing her heart-shaped face. "Girl, you won't believe what happened!"

"Tell me, don't make me beat it out of you."

She laughs. "Oh, you're gonna love this." Rachel leans forward, her eyes sparkling with mischief. "So, you know Mark, right? The one with that crazy obsession for artisanal cheese and rollerblading in his underwear?"

"That is *disgusting*," I say deadpan. "Please continue."

"He's at the farmer's market, doing his usual cheese-sampling routine, when he spots this huge wheel of Camembert. Like, it's practically the size of his head!"

My laughter erupts, and I cover my mouth with my hand, imagining the absurdity of the situation. "No way!"

"Oh, yes way." Rachel nods, her eyes dancing. "So, he decides he must conquer this Camembert mountain, right? He's determined to finish the whole thing, like a cheese gladiator. Fucking creep."

I can barely breathe through my laughter, envisioning Mark in a cheese-eating battle of epic proportions.

"But here's the kicker." Rachel leans in. "Turns out that Camembert was like... super potent. The stinkiest cheese known to humankind and I mean rancid."

Fuck, this is too funny. I burst into another fit of laughter, imagining poor Mark unwittingly subjecting himself to the cheese equivalent of a taste bud assault.

"And there he is," Rachel continues, "cheeks flushed, eyes watering, as he tries to conquer this cheese monster. People are giving him a wide berth like he's a ticking time bomb of cheese-induced aroma."

"This story is sick, Rach, and I bet you watched it all, you bastard!" I'm laughing so hard, my stomach hurts.

"Damn right, I did. Long story short," Rachel concludes, "he didn't conquer the Camembert. The Camembert conquered him. He ended up running away, defeated by dairy."

"I think I just threw up in my mouth."

"Me too!"

We both dissolve into giggles, our sides aching and tears streaming down our faces. This crazy bitch! It's moments like these when Rachel's storytelling prowess meets my penchant for ridiculous scenarios that remind me why her friendship is worth more than all the cheese wheels in the world. Our laughter dies down, and I sigh through my nose, taking her hand in mine. "How are you, really? You never visit me here in Willowdale. How are your parents?"

The smile on my face fades. "They're around..." Fuck if I know where. "I haven't spoken to them in almost a year."

Rachel knows better than anyone how hard Shane's suicide was on my family. My mother closed herself off completely and my father retreated deeper into his work. It got to the point where we barely spoke, and I was spending more time at Rachel's and Blake's houses than my own.

"Are you going to be okay seeing him?" Rachel asks, with a melancholic stare.

*Fuck.* She always knows what to say to make my eyes burn. I nod, but don't respond to that. It's in the past. Blake and I are different people, though. Since high school, I've had several relationships and it's been five years since we broke up. I'm sure he's moved on. "Besides, I'm almost positive he's fat and bald by now anyway, with nine kids, jerking off to gay porn every night."

She gives me a pitying smile and squeezes my hand.

And as I sit there, surrounded by the sweet scent of baked goods and the warmth of Rachel's friendship, I realize that maybe, just maybe, this reunion won't be the nightmare I anticipated. With Rachel by my side, even the darkest corners of my past seem a little less daunting.

She brushes a few stray strands of my thick, brown, curly hair away from my eyes, her touch soothing in its familiarity. My gaze drifts to the TV mounted in the corner where a hockey game is playing. My face lights up immediately, drawn to the sight of the sport I've always loved.

"Speaking of him...guess who's making waves in the NHL?"

I blink at her. "Who?"

"Blake Bryan."

I frown, my excitement faltering for a moment. "So, he's not fat and bald?"

"He's not fat and bald, Kieran," she replies, chuckling. "He's actually the best defenseman for the Detroit Red Wings. Can you believe it?"

My jaw drops, and I nearly choke on the bite of the muffin I was about to take. *Shit.* I feel my face flushing as thoughts of Blake resurface like a ghost from the past. Damn. I thought I'd get revenge on him by turning up looking smoking hot, but I can't do that if he's also a stud. *Would he remember me? Does it matter?* I remind myself that I'm not that same vulnerable teenager anymore. *I'm a successful, confident, capable, independent man, dammit!*

I snort, pretending nonchalance even as my heart races. "Well, well, look at him go. From closeted jock to NHL superstar closeted jock. Good for him."

Rachel, the villain, laughs at my theatrics. "Oh, Kieran, your act could win you an Oscar. Just admit it, the thought of him stirs something in you."

"Yeah, my indigestion," I mutter.

"Bitch please, I can practically see your hard-on underneath the table."

I narrow my eyes at her, half-tempted to stick my tongue out like a child. "Frankly, I don't know what you're talking about. Blake Bryan is ancient history. I've got better things to do than think about him."

She leans back in her chair. "Sure, Kieran. Whatever you say."

"Say that again and I'll beat you to death with my blueberry muffin."

\*\*\*

"Seriously?" Rachel clings to my arms like an octopus as I struggle to hail a cab. "Just stay at my place. Why are you making things so complicated?"

"Your entire family from Michigan is descending upon you," I chuckle. "And as much as I adore your parents, you know how those 'are you sure you're not gay' comments tend to pile up during the holidays. I don't think I have enough patience for the interrogation this year."

"*Kieran*," she whines, pouting her lips. "Please. I need you with me."

"For God's sake, pull yourself together, woman!" I say, pinching her cheek. "You'll be fine without me."

Rachel's earnest eyes plead with me to stay at her place, a plea she's delivered countless times before. But the solitude of my own space calls to me. I offer her a reassuring smile. "Don't worry, Rach. I'll be okay at the cabin. You know how much I value my alone time."

She pouts playfully, but there's genuine concern in her gaze. "Alright, just promise me you'll text me if you need anything, okay?"

"Promise," I assure her, giving her a quick hug before waving goodbye. With that, I head towards the waiting cab that will take me to my parents' cabin up in the woods. The drive is serene, winding through snow-dusted trees and rolling hills. There are so many memories here, both good and bad, but I heave a deep sigh, relaxing in my seat. The cab drops me off at a quaint bungalow perched on a hilltop, with large windows that offer a panoramic view of the surrounding forest. The air is crisp and invigorating, and the scent of pine fills my senses. The cottage itself is a cozy haven, furnished with simple elegance, everything covered in white blankets as if to preserve everything from the past.

As I step inside, a sense of nostalgia washes over me. This was our refuge, mine and my brother Shane's hideout. We used to love it here, spending hours exploring the woods, playing by the fireplace, and pretending we were kings of our own little kingdom. But after his death, my parents never returned, leaving this place frozen in time.

*Shane.* I lift a photograph from the dresser, my gaze locked onto it as a cascade of memories resurfaces. In the picture, Shane and I stand shoulder to shoulder, both of us navigating the delicate art of ice skating. He flashes a radiant grin, donning a hockey jersey as though it were a badge of honor.

Shane had big dreams. He wanted to be a hockey star like the famous legends Gretzky, Lemieux, Orr, and Howe. I wanted to be great at skating too, to make a name for myself. We both had these dreams and shared them back then when we were young. But all of those dreams fell apart when Shane took his own life. We were like two peas in a pod, so similar in height, age, and what we wanted. We were supposed to achieve our dreams together. But now those dreams are shattered and gone. The heaviness of Shane not being here is something I've carried with me. It's like a scar on my heart.

In the picture, we look so innocent, like close brothers. It's strange to think about that happy smile and then what actually happened later. About a year before he left us, Shane changed. He became distant, his laughs disappearing. He tried to hide his anger and sadness behind a fake smile.

I shake my head as if attempting to erase the heartrending memories etched into my mind. The night he left, I returned home to the anguished cries of my mother, a sound that still echoes in the corridors of my soul. Shane had hung himself in his room.

"Fuck," I whisper, putting the picture back down.

Some days, the pain feels as strong as when it all happened. On other days, it's a constant ache that never really goes away. I often wonder if we missed any signs or subtle hints that we didn't catch because we were so busy.

But regrets just make things worse. So, I take a deep breath and start doing things around the cabin. I light up the fireplace, and the crackling fire makes the room feel cozy. I check what food I have and make a mental list of what to buy. I'm not staying for too long, just a weekend maybe before I have to go back to my busy life in Los Angeles.

Just as I'm settling in, there's a knock on the door. I open it to find Jason, the groundsman, standing there dressed in sturdy winter clothes. His friendly smile is a welcome sight as we shake hands. He's an older gentleman with light blonde hair streaked with white. His eyes twinkle as he wipes the fallen snow off his broad shoulders. "Hey, Kieran. It's been a while."

"Yeah, it has," I reply, genuinely glad to see him. "How's the family?"

Jason's pale blue eyes brighten. "They're good. The kids are growing up fast, you know how it is. Everything's taken care of around here, just like you wanted. I just came by to see if you need anything else for your stay here this weekend."

I nod, a small weight lifting off my shoulders. "Thanks, Jason. I appreciate it, but I'm good for now."

"No problem at all. You enjoy your time here," he says before heading off.

With the cabin in good hands, I text Rachel, asking her to bring over some groceries and sending her the money through an e-transfer. I pour myself another shot of whisky, not because I'm an alcoholic, but because the anticipation of seeing Blake has my stomach tied in knots.

I switch on the TV to ESPN just as the hockey game is about the begin—the Boston Bruins against the New York Rangers. I'm by no means a superfan, but there's something about the sport that draws me in. Slinking down onto the couch, I try to let go of all my thoughts and relax, but suddenly, I'm transported back in time to the days when Blake taught me how to skate, his patience and laughter echoing in my memory. The game becomes a bridge to the past, reminding me of who I used to be before everything changed.

***

*SKATING ON ICE TURNS out to be my personal slapstick comedy. My knees and elbows seem to think they're doing some kind of ice dance routine – just not the one I had in mind. Blake's laughter echoes across the frozen landscape, like background music to my hilarious misadventures.*

*"Kieran, you're a natural," he quips, clearly enjoying the show.*

*I give him my best mock glare, huffing as I pick myself up, again. "Yeah, right. I'm the undisputed king of icy acrobatics."*

*In comes Blake, skating over like he's auditioning for a figure skating championship. "Let me show you how the pros do it," he declares, swooping in to rescue me from my own clumsiness. His gloved hand steadies me, providing a warm contrast to the frosty chaos.*

*As he guides me – or rather, drags me – across the rink, something shifts. The world slows down, and for a moment, it feels like a scene from a romantic movie. Not a very graceful one, mind you. More like a rom-com blooper reel.*

*And then, the universe decides to throw us an ice curveball. My feet decide to dance a jig of their own, and Blake, in a heroic act of solidarity, joins me in a synchronized slip-and-slide. We land in a heap of tangled limbs, laughing and yelping like kids on a playground. Our eyes meet, and I can't help but laugh even harder.*

*With a classic comedic twist, Blake positions himself above me, his hair falling in his eyes like a rebellious curtain. I can feel the warmth of his proximity, and my face heats up faster than a microwave burrito. "Yeah, I might have missed my calling as an ice dancer," I joke, trying to keep my cool amidst the frosty situation.*

*Then, in a plot twist I definitely didn't see coming, Blake inches closer. His lips, thankfully not frozen to the touch, press against mine. It's like a scene from a cheesy romance movie, except we're on ice and I'm pretty sure my nose is bright red from the cold.*

*But before I can process what's happening, he pulls away, his words tripping over each other in a hurry. His face looks like a tomato that just found out it's in a salad. And naturally, my face must match the tomato's color chart.*

*"You—You suck so much I had to kiss you to make you feel better," Blake stutters.*

*"Yeah. Right."*

*I'm shocked into silence, my mouth still tingling. Blake and I lock eyes and before either of us can blink, we are both surging forward again.*

*I'm not sure when exactly we fell in love, but I fell hard and couldn't stop it. Blake means everything to me. Because my parents ignore me, Blake and Rachel are the only ones in my life. When he kisses me for the first time, it feels like everything shakes and breaks into pieces. The first time we're together intimately, it's so intense that I think my heart might explode. Blake is so gentle, and being with him makes me sure that he's the one I want to be with for life. Even when things are crazy, he's the steady thing. I really want to be in his arms forever.*

*Senior year is a whirlwind. We have moments like this where we talk about secrets and dreams, and when it's just us and the ice, the world feels small. Back then, I only imagined a future with Blake.*

*But one night changes everything. The crowd is loud and excited, and I'm focused on every move of the game. Blake's energy is electric, and when he scores the winning goal, everyone goes wild.*

*I'm eager to get to him, my heart beating fast. I burst into the locker room, my face wet with happy tears. He's there, surrounded by friends, his jersey half off.*

*"Blake!" I'm shaky, but bold with pride and excitement. I try to hug him, wrapping my arms around him. He's sweaty, still in his gear, breathing heavily. I'm pouring out my love and happiness.*

*He turns to me, surprise turning into discomfort. His friends exchange looks, and he moves away from my touch. Then he says something that bursts my happiness.*

*"I know you have feelings for me, but is this really the time?" His tone is mocking, his laughter cruel as he looks at me like I'm a joke. "Goddamn fag."*

*I freeze. Everything around me feels off. My face is hot, and his words hit me hard. I feel like everyone's staring like I'm on display. I can't breathe or think. All I can do is get away.*

*Tears fill my eyes, and I can't see well. Feeling embarrassed and broken, I leave the locker room without a word, leaving behind the person who broke my heart.*

\*\*\*

THE BITTER MEMORIES ARE like an open wound, refusing to heal. They are a constant reminder, like a tattoo etched in my mind. Seriously, thanks a lot, Blake. You've earned a prime spot in my gallery of painful experiences. *Bravo*.

Shifting in my seat, I clutch my glass as if it holds all the answers. Well, it contains whiskey, which is pretty close, right? The alcohol burns going down, but not as much as the memory of that night. I have Blake to thank for making me wary of trusting anyone who hasn't fully embraced their true selves. Closeted asshole.

Glaring at the TV, the hockey game plays on, completely unaware that it's the backdrop to my brewing plan for revenge. *Skate your hearts out, while I hatch a scheme that could rival those from spy novels.*

The plan had been hatched over a drink, or three, a few weeks ago when Rachel and I had decided that Blake's closet doors needed some vigorous opening. *Metaphorically, of course.* Although a part of me was tempted to fly in there with a rainbow cape and some confetti cannons.

But I digress.

I smirk into my empty glass. Not this time, Blake. This time, it's me with the upper hand, or, well, the touchscreen. Because in this digital age, I am going to hit you where it hurts—your carefully curated public image.

With a devious grin, I place the goblet down with a bit more force than necessary. I mean, I wasn't in a movie, but if I were, this would be my 'villain plotting' scene.

I grab my phone, thumbs flying across the screen like a pianist possessed by Beethoven. Or in my case, possessed by sheer determination to get sweet, sweet payback. The text message to Rachel is simple and direct, though humorously cryptic: *Operation: Un-Closet the Closet. Are you in?* I laugh remembering the day she came to visit me and we put everything together.

\*\*\*

*"So, Rachel, here's the master plan."* I hiccup, bending down to sip *my fifth Mojito for the night. "I think it's about time my high school sweetheart comes out of the closet. But, we'll do it with flair."*

*"That sounds unnecessarily complicated, but please continue."* Rachel *raises an eyebrow. "I'm listening. What's the first step?"*

*"Well, step one is all about the art of infiltration,"* I said, trying to *hold back a mischievous grin. "We'll reach out through an alias that's so convincing, Blake won't suspect a thing. Alternatively, we can use our network of mutual friends who are blissfully unaware of our past."*

*Rachel nods, getting into the spirit of the plan. "And what's next?"*

*"Now, here's where it gets really interesting,"* I continued. *"We'll subtly manipulate our conversations and craft situations that'll make Blake question his choices. Think of it as a gentle nudge in the right direction. Plus, we'll sprinkle in hints about LGBTQ+ individuals living their best lives to create a bit of internal turmoil."*

*Rachel chuckles. "You're devious. What's the grand finale?"*

*"Then, I'll orchestrate a public reveal, exposing Blake's secret to a wider audience. He'll have no choice but to come out—"*

*"And you've lost me."*

*"It's the perfect plan!"* I finish enthusiastically.

*"Yeah, if you want to cause irreversible damage,"* Rachel responds *with a hint of concern.*

*"But Rach—"* I whine.

*"Alright, no more Mojitos for you. Can we get the bill, please?"* Rachel *signals to the waiter, clearly deciding it's time to wrap up our conversation.*

*"Then what should I do?"* I pout, feeling a little deflated.

*Rachel looks at me, her big brown eyes softening. "Look, if you want Blake to come out, just tell him how you feel. You might be surprised by the outcome."*

*I doubt it. No, I can't abandon Operation: Un-Closet the Closet entirely.*

*I just need to modify it a bit.*

***

MY CELLPHONE BEEPS with her enthusiastic response and a parade of emojis that includes rainbows, magnifying glasses, and a sparkly thumbs-up. My partner in crime is locked and loaded. Our payback-fueled quest is a go.

As I lean back, the TV still blaring, I realize this was my moment. Revenge was a dish best served cold, and right now I am an iceberg in the Arctic. With a confident grin, I raise an imaginary toast to Blake's inevitable exposure, watching the hockey game with newfound interest.

The game is about to change. And I am the one holding the joystick.

## 2

---·---

# THAWING WALLS, RISING HEAT

I step into the familiar halls of my old high school, dressed to the nines in a crisp black suit that's as sharp as a freshly minted banknote. My black slacks and shirt create a sleek silhouette, while my carefully styled brown hair flops over my brow with a hint of gel-enhanced nonchalance. *Okay fine. I might have indulged in a drink or five before coming in, but who's keeping count?* The fact that the floor seems to have decided it wants to play spin-the-world isn't exactly a priority right now. Besides, is that SpongeBob over there? Oh, wait, no, it's just my gym teacher, Mr. Grains. Note to self: Perhaps cutting off at drink number four would have been wise.

The theme is "Winter Wonderland," but my enthusiasm for the icy extravaganza hit a frosty wall the moment Rachel revealed her dress. Ice blue and sparkling, it's like she's single-handedly trying to turn herself into an ice sculpture. Seriously, there's so much ice on that dress it could blind an astronaut in outer space. But hey, it's Rachel, and she owns every glittering sequin of it. So, arm in arm, we saunter into the building, my stylish façade slightly swaying but still holding strong.

My main bitch and I make a beeline for the fruit punch table, eyes scanning the room as we approach. Faces from the past and the present blend together, some recognizable, others transformed by the cruel march of time. It's like a living yearbook, complete with wrinkles and graying hair. I catch glimpses of people who once filled these hallways with laughter and drama, now gathered for this grand reunion.

"So, who do you see in the crowd, Kieran?" Rachel nudges me, a twinkle in her eye as she holds her cup of punch. Her dress might be blinding, but her smile is infectious.

I take another sip of the punch, the sugar rush and a hint of nostalgia hitting me all at once. "Oh, you know, the usual suspects. There's Mark Stillman, looking like he's about to give a TED Talk, and Jenny Simmons, who seems to have swapped her cheerleader uniform for a power suit. And then, of course, there's Mr. Grains, who I could've sworn was SpongeBob for a second there."

Rachel chuckles, shaking her head. "Leave it to you to turn our reunion into a sitcom. But hey, at least you're keeping things entertaining."

I raise an eyebrow at her playfully. "Entertaining? Me? Never."

As I glance around, I can't help but smile. The years might have changed us, but the essence of those high school days—full of dreams, insecurities, and a touch of teenage angst—still lingers.

"Fuck, times have changed," I mumble. Most of the cheerleaders who used to turn heads now seem to have turned into walking sacks of potatoes. I mean, I'm all for embracing a comfort-first fashion approach, but these folks are channeling the humble spud a bit too literally. Trying to contain my snickers, I'm silently judging their transformation. Who knew a "Winter Wonderland" theme could lead to such starchy fashion choices?

Just as I'm thoroughly entertaining myself with the potato parade, a hand the size of a baseball mitt lands a congratulatory thump on my back. "Kieran? Kieran Hunter?" The voice is hearty, the familiarity jolting me from my amusement. I pivot, and there he stands, all hulking presence and contagious grin. Miles Butterbutt—scratch that—Miles the Mountain. Seriously, he's morphed into a Dwayne "The Rock" Johnson look-alike. Delicious. I could climb him like a fucking tree.

"Miles?" I greet, my voice half an octave too high thanks to my surprise.

His grin widens, and he gives me a firm handshake that feels like I'm being introduced to a steel vise. "Well, look who's all dressed up and causing a commotion."

I glance down at my suit, feeling a touch self-conscious despite the fact that I look like a GQ model had a love child with James Bond's wardrobe. "Well, I figured if I was going to subject myself to this madness, I might as well do it in style."

"You've always had a way with words, Kieran." Miles lets out a hearty laugh that probably resonates through the building. Fuck, it goes straight through my spine. If I wasn't hard before, I'm certainly half-hard now.

I clear my throat. "Do you remember Rachel—"

"Swan," Miles drawls, and they shake hands. "How could I forget? Didn't you stomp on Taylor's balls for trying to grope you in the cafeteria?"

Rachel grins wickedly. "One of my finest moments, if I do say so myself."

"I'm pretty sure he had to have testicle reconstruction surgery," Miles mused. "Damn, that shit was crazy."

I'm blinded by his pearly white teeth, and I'm about to tell Rachel to get lost so I can have my way with this NFL God when she beats me to it. "Oh, look, it's Shelia—she owes me for beating up her neighbor for trying to harass her, excuse me." Then she's off, shoving through the crowd.

I laugh as my eyes trail after her, shaking my head.

"Some things never change," Miles says, dragging his large thumb over his plump bottom lip.

"Man, catching up like this brings back memories," I say, taking a sip of my drink.

Miles nods, a grin spreading across his face. "No kidding. Remember the unholy trinity—me, you, and Rachel?"

I chuckle, shaking my head. "Oh, how could I forget? We were quite the trio."

Miles leans in, his voice dropping to a seductive tone. "And look at us now. Who would've thought? From being the target of bullies to me becoming an NFL linebacker for the Detroit Pistons."

*Take me to church, Daddy.* Heat flares over my cheeks. I raise an eyebrow, playfully incredulous. "Seriously? It's like a sports movie, just with way more protein shakes."

Miles laughs, his eyes wrinkling. His tall nose is straight, followed by phoenix eyes and pink lips. His skin is fairer than Rachel's, smooth like a crisp autumn leaf. I'm sure his cock is just as pretty.

"So, what have you been up to?" Miles asks, his grin equal parts charming and mischievous.

I take a sip of punch, avoiding the temptation to spill it in surprise. "Oh, you know, the usual. I've become a professional pet food taster."

"No way, you're kidding!" Miles snorts. "How the hell did you get into that?"

"I entered a 'Guess the Mystery Flavor' contest for pet treats and won four times in a row. At that point, I knew I had a talent for deciphering flavors that even dogs and cats couldn't resist. My friends suggested I put my taste buds to good use."

Miles blinks at me. "Are you serious?"

I laugh. "Fuck no, I just did it because they pay me a lot of money."

He laughs so hard that I'm half-convinced he's going to need medical attention. "Kieran Hunter, the pet food connoisseur. That's a good one."

I'm just about to respond when the doors swing open, and there he is, walking in with an air of quiet confidence that commands attention. Blake Bryan. My history, my heartbreak, my personal vendetta. The boy who crushed my soul.

***

DAMN, THERE HE GOES, striding into the room like he owns it. Blake Bryan, or should I say Mr. Heartthrob Extraordinaire, like a charismatic movie star, effortlessly stealing the spotlight. *He's not fat or bald. I want to scream to the heavens.* Blake's broad shoulders, accentuated by a well-fitted three-piece tux, seem to belong on a runway more than in a high school reunion. A trail of his former jock minions follows behind him, in awe and worship. *Seriously, I think a few hearts just palpitated out of sync.* His lip ring glitters in the strobe lights, the piercing green eyes and that rebellious thick wavy black hair adding extra exclamation marks. My knees decide they have a newfound penchant for being jelly, and I'm pretty sure I just invented a shade of red that's never existed as my face burns up.

Oh, joy. He and I lock eyes, and it's like the universe is playing a cosmic prank on me.

My survival instincts kick in, and I take a fortifying sip from my drink, hoping it will magically transform into a shield of invisibility. *Operation: Un-Closet the Closet? Yeah, it's officially underway.*

Just as I'm about to drift away into the conversation Miles is having about gym routines and biceps, my gaze swerves back like a rubber band pulled taut. Blake is surrounded, a gravitational force drawing on every curious onlooker and eager fan. A cascade of admirers all but beg for autographs, their adoration in stark contrast to my internal eye-roll.

"Hey, big fan here! Can I get an autograph?" A starry-eyed individual swoops in, thrusting a pen and paper toward Miles. Apparently, being an NFL linebacker has its perks, even at a high school reunion.

Miles shoots me an apologetic look. "Duty calls," he says and turns to the fan.

As they chat away, I attempt to distract myself with the allure of my drink. Unfortunately, distraction levels are at an all-time low when I feel a warm hand glide down my back, meaty fingers settling on my hip. A shiver races down my spine, and I'm pretty sure my drink just turned into the world's least effective fire extinguisher.

"Hey there, remember me?" a low voice whispers in my ear, brushing hot against my earlobe.

*Blake.* My heart rate kicks up to a NASCAR-worthy speed. *Sexual harassment much?* My body jerks away from the warmth of his touch, the sensation setting off an internal alarm. I pivot, perhaps a bit too sharply, to face him. His gaze remains steady, and I can practically feel my cheeks burning with a blush that betrays my momentary vulnerability. I'm not short by any means, but Blake towers over my 5'11 frame. He's 6'1 and built like an Ford F-150.

"You'll have to jog my memory," I lie smoothly. "The reunion is playing havoc with my recollections, you know."

"Sorry, I didn't mean to startle you," he offers, his voice carrying a note of sincere apology.

I manage to conjure a semblance of a smile, my efforts to play it cool practically visible in the air. "No big deal. Just a bit jumpy tonight, I guess. How've you been?"

His eyes, cool and searching, seem to dissect me layer by layer, causing a warmth that has nothing to do with embarrassment to flood my cheeks. "Good," he replies, his voice carrying a hint of something I can't quite place. "I'm good."

I nod, attempting to mask my lingering discomfort with a casual demeanor. "So, you made it to the NFL. Congratulations."

Blake snorts, a genuine smile crossing his face. "Yeah, bro. It's been quite the ride." As he licks his lips, his tongue circles his lip ring in a nervous gesture. My brain short-circuits. *Fuck me*. I clear my throat, my thoughts running a marathon without my permission. "Hey, do you want to get out of here?"

"Now?" I asked incredulously. *He just got here.* But his eyes are heavy-lidded and his gaze pierces mine. Oh. *Oh*. His proposal is swift, and it takes a second for my brain to catch up. *So fast? At least buy me a drink before sweeping me off my feet.* My heart races, and before I can assess the pros and cons of the situation, I find myself saying yes. Nice job, Kieran. You're apparently cheaper than a four-dollar hooker. He doesn't wait for a response.

With a subtle touch, Blake's fingers graze my elbow, and he guides me towards the exit. I catch Rachel's disapproving glance, a silent 'Hoes before bros' that makes me internally groan. Sorry! I shoot back with a helpless glance, mentally promising her a play-by-play later.

*** 

THE WINTRY AIR OUTSIDE greets us with a bruising slap, a stark contrast to the lingering warmth of the reunion hall. Blake guides me to a corner, and the intensity in his eyes is impossible to ignore. Something's different about him. He steps closer, and it's in that proximity that I detect the tremor in his usually confident demeanor. Nervous, really nervous. The hand on my arm burns and I feel a shiver roll through me as I gaze up at him.

Blake's messy black waves cascade effortlessly over his forehead, a tempting curtain that frames his face. His green eyes are like shards of glass, locked onto mine. *God damn, that piercing.* I remember sucking on it for hours, pulling his pink yet soft lips, and rolling them between my teeth.

I couldn't deny the magnetic pull, even if I wanted to. Blake looks down at me, his breath a wispy fog between us, and he chuckles, his deep baritone voice making me shudder.

"Now that I've seen you again, I don't know what to say."

Neither do I, but I can't speak. Instead, I swallow around the blockage in my throat.

"Look." He steps closer, and a base note of the rich sandalwood of his aftershave clings to the air like it had a personal invitation. Fuck, it's making my dick hard. "I've been wanting to say this for years, but I never had the chance to."

"Say what?" I breathe, practically dizzy from how close he is.

"I'm sorry. For how I treated you back then. I was an asshole, and I regret it every day—"

He starts speaking, and for a moment, his words sound like a foreign language I can't decipher. And then I can't help it. A laugh escapes my lips. *It has to be a joke, right?* Blake Bryan, the guy who once made my life a living hell, is apologizing? No way.

"It's cool, man," I reply, my attempt at nonchalance more successful than I feel. "High school, right? Water under the bridge."

"Really? You're not harboring some secret vendetta to suffocate me in my sleep? Because if it'll make you feel better, I'll totally let you." His raised eyebrow questions my response.

"Well... it would make for an interesting headline. 'Man Suffocates Former Bully with Pillow, Claims Nostalgia as Motive.'"

We both laugh. "Nah, seriously, man. I'm good. It was so long ago, I'd forgotten it."

*Not really. And if I stayed up every single night for the last five years plotting his death, he doesn't need to know.*

Blake's face lights up, and he takes a step closer, his fingers brushing mine. "Good. Great. I'm not that guy anymore, I promise, Kieran."

*Whatever. I hope that the closet is big enough for all of Narnia.*

I've changed? Yeah right. It's a bold statement, and I want to challenge it. The ghosts of the past are too fresh to ignore, but Operation: Un-Closet the Closet is still very much the main act here. So, I hold my tongue, my insides churning like a blender on overdrive. This conversation is painful, and I'm itching to change the subject. *Why couldn't he have changed back then?* I turn my face away, unwilling to go down that path. Time to put him to the test. I purse my lips and then lean forward. Blake's throat bobs, his green eyes tracking the long pale column of my throat. *A place he used to suck on for hours.*

"Really?" I drawl, closing the space between us just a tad. "Well, I'm staying at my parents' cabin. How about you swing by? Maybe after this? We can catch up like old times...and you can show me just how *much* you've changed."

Blake's pupils dilate. It's quick and strident. Desire. He's tempted, I can tell. And for the first time tonight, I feel a spark of triumph. Kieran: 1, Homophobe: 0. Blake's face reddens slightly, his gaze momentarily locking on my lips before he clears his throat. "Yeah. Sure. Let me, uh, tell my friends, and we can head over."

I watch him walk away, sighing at the way his slacks cling to his sculpted ass. *Fuck, tonight was going to be good. Operation: Un-Closet the Closet* is in motion.

*** 

THE RIDE BACK TO THE cabin with Blake is quiet, but it's as if the air itself is charged with an unspoken tension. I'm bundled up in layers, my coat draped over my thick black jacket, and he's got his own bundled attire going on. Blake's white Mercedes Benz pulls up to the cabin, stopping in the familiar spot that used to be his. I swallow down the lump in my throat, pushing aside the rush of emotions as we both step out of the car and head inside.

I flick on the lights, shedding my coat and immediately making a beeline for the fireplace. The cold still lingers in the cabin, and I'm eager for warmth to envelop the space. In the kitchen, I start making hot cocoa, the sound of the clinking mugs offering a momentary distraction from the whirlwind of emotions I'm trying to suppress.

Blake settles onto the couch with an ease that speaks of familiarity. I bring over the mugs, and his gaze lingers on the kitten mug in my hand. "It was the only mug we had left."

"Yeah, I remember this mug. It used to be...my mug. Remember?"

A pang of guilt tugs at me as I realize I'd forgotten about that. I offer a sheepish smile, memories flooding back. "Right, yeah. Sorry about that."

We sit down, side by side, each cradling a mug of hot cocoa. Blake's eyes catch a glimpse of the broken edge of the table. "You never got that fixed?"

I shake my head. "Nah, I kept it for the memories."

"Yeah, I remember the time we thought we could be the next Lemieux. I slapped my stick so hard it went right through the kitchen window. My soul left my body when your mom walked in."

The memory hits me like a wave, and I can't help but burst into laughter. "Oh god, yeah. I remember that. Time really does fly, doesn't it?"

"Shit man, there are so many memories. It's screwing with my head," he says. "Regrets too..." he adds with a forlorn expression before he perks up. "Hey, remember when we watched the Chicago Blackhawks take on the Boston Bruins?"

I chuckle, that memory flashing before me like a vivid picture. "Oh, absolutely, dude."

"The Blackhawks had Toews and Kane tearing up the ice," Blake reminisces. "Yeah, and the Bruins had Bergeron leading the charge, with Chara's towering presence guarding the net."

"Remember that overtime? The tension was insane."

Blake's eyes flash with excitement. "And then that slapshot from the blue line, and the Bruins took the win."

"Oh man, I made some serious noise when that happened."

He shoves me playfully. "No kidding. I thought you'd wake up the whole neighborhood."

I laugh even harder. "Well, you know, a Bruins victory calls for some celebration."

"And I thought we could actually watch a game without your legendary shouts."

"Hey, it's not a real game if I'm not shouting like a maniac. Adds to the charm, don't you think?"

"Yeah, you're right. Wouldn't have it any other way," Blake says. "No, scratch that. I think I would." He gazes at me intently. "I think I'd rather have you shouting like that while I fuck you."

I choke on my hot cocoa, my face flaming red. "Jesus, Blake."

"What?" He inches closer. "You don't want it?"

*You know I do.* The words are at the tip of my tongue and my heart slams against my chest when his large hands slide up my thigh. I'm rock hard in seconds. The weight of the years melts away, leaving behind a sense of comfort that's oddly familiar, like slipping into a well-worn sweater. Blake. Fucking Blake. He leans forward, his black scuff grazing my cheek. "How about I take you here, and you can scream my name just like you used to?"

*Well, how can I say no to that?*

# 3

— . —

## EMBERS OF CHANGE IGNITE

The crackling fire transforms the room into a cozy haven, its flickering glow casting dancing shadows on the walls. Blake and I share the couch, close enough that I can practically feel the heat of his body. Fuck, this trip has been a whirlwind, and I don't know how I'll survive when I return to my life in LA. For most of my life, Blake had been my world, and it had shattered the moment he rejected me. Rejected us.

Suddenly, in what feels like a scene stolen from a cheesy romance movie, Blake's hand finds mine, and our fingers intertwine in a surprisingly seamless fit. It's like our hands were secretly best friends this whole time. My heart skips a beat or three.

*Okay, the mixtape of my emotions has hit shuffle mode.*

Our eyes meet, and in his gaze, there's an unmistakable question. It's the kind of question that can only be answered with a kiss. Like an actor hitting their mark, Blake leans in. I'm torn between feeling like a character in a romantic novel and wondering if I should've brought popcorn. My knees turn to jelly and all the emotions from earlier come rushing back.

His lips graze mine, and it's like the universe just synchronized its playlist to play our song. Our lips meet, a soft collision that quickly escalates to a full-blown orchestra of sensations. Blake's lips are as smooth and inviting as I remember, and his beard bristles against my skin.

"Kieran," he whispers, and my stomach clenches.

My cock is hard and erect, begging for attention. Soon, our lips are performing a synchronized tango that'd put Dancing with the Stars to shame. There's a tentative exploration that quickly evolves into a full-on invasion of personal lip space. But hey, I'm not complaining. The fire's flickering like it's trying to keep up with our chemistry.

Blake's hand cradles my cheek while my hand apparently morphed into a magnet and can't seem to let go of his chest. His heart beats under my palm, like a subtle reminder that this isn't a dream sequence—*I'm here, and I'm not going anywhere.* Fuck, I shouldn't want him as badly as I do.

Time goes all Inception on us as minutes feel like seconds and hours like minutes. Our lips continue their gravity-defying routine, and I realize that I'm not just kissing him—I'm tasting memories and dreams we never dared to chase. Blake. *My best friend. My first love.*

The fire, probably wondering if it's in the right story, adds its own commentary with a hearty crackle. And as the flames light up the room, it's like they're winking at us, saying, "You got this, smoochers."

As the kiss takes on a life of its own, emotions whirl within me. It's a dizzying cocktail of nostalgia, longing, and a dash of "holy crap, this is actually happening."

Blake yanks away, his face flushing, his large thumb brushing over my jawline. "Fuck, Kieran."

*My thoughts exactly.* Breaths mingling, I can't help but chuckle. Because if kissing Blake feels like this, then sign me up for a repeat performance—a sequel, a trilogy, heck, let's make it a franchise. The fire, clearly approving of our chemistry, throws in a final flourish, and

I realize that this moment is the stuff cheesy movies are made of. But who needs movies when you've got your own star-studded scene right here by the fire?

"Do you want me?" Blake asks breathlessly. "Tell me to stop."

"Never." We're past the point of no return. I shove him onto the plush fur rug and straddle his hips, ready to unleash my inner cowgirl, when he grabs my narrow waist, moaning long and loud. The 'point of no return' is now merely a distant speck in our rearview mirror as he grabs my neck and pulls me down on top of him, covering my mouth with a bruising kiss. *Fuck yes!*

I jerk my hips, groaning when I feel Blake's thick cock through his slacks. The delicious heat between us is enough to make my toes curl. His muscles are thick and corded in his jacket. I want to lick him from head to toe like an ice cream cone. "Blake," I gasp into his mouth.

He grunts and then snakes his hands between our bodies as I writhe on top of him, and he starts to fumble with the button of my slacks, wrenching it open. "Damn, Kieran. You taste so fucking good."

The adrenaline is pumping through my veins as I fumble with the buttons on his shirt and lift it over his head, and I can't help but notice the way he trembles as my fingers brush over his chest.

"I've waited so long for you," Blake murmurs, but his voice is taut. "I'm sorry. So sorry."

My brain is in a lust-induced fog, so I can't really make out what he's saying so I do the same thing and ignore it. Talking about the past is too painful. I'd rather lose myself in the desire.

With his shirt swiftly thrown to the floor, I pull him towards me to resume our fevered kiss. The contact of his now bare chest on mine is exhilarating in the best way possible. Blake breaks the kiss, and I swear the room is spinning as his hands grip my shoulders, and he's rolling us until I'm on my back, staring up into his dark eyes as he pins me to the mattress. He moves down on the rug in one fluid motion to kneel by my feet, his eyes never leaving mine.

Blake dips his fingers below the waistband of my slacks and gently tugs, sending the fabric sliding past my hips and down my legs before he carelessly throws them on the floor. A small smile plays across his face as he sees I'm wearing nothing else underneath, but it quickly vanishes, only to be replaced with a look of utter adoration. "Commando? Really?"

"You know I have a condition that makes me allergic to certain types of fabrics!" I say back, my face flushing red.

He looks at me like I'm everything he's ever wanted but never thought he could have. His fingers trail up my leg, just barely making contact, like he's scared to touch me for fear of finding out I'm not really here, lying in front of him. I grab his hand and pull him within inches of my face, whispering with my gaze burning into his. The words are for me as much as they are for him.

"This is real. I never thought...Kieran..."

He traces his fingers along my jawline, and the way Blake's fingers ghost over my skin, it's like he's trying to banish the ghosts of the past. I run my fingers down his sides until I'm gently tugging at the elastic band of his pants, signaling my wants. Blake's lips cover mine again as he moves to shed his pants and boxers, without ever breaking the kiss. He flips me onto my back, knocking the wind out of me, and then pulls away and hovers his lips above mine, whispering in a tone that's low and heavy. "Last chance to call this off."

"What is this, 21 questions? You need to learn to take 'yes' for an answer. I want this."

Blake grunts, capturing my mouth in a searing kiss. I groan as his hot mouth leaves a wet trail down my neck before going to my torso. My hips jerk as Blake's lips ghost over my hipbones.

I forget my name when I feel them envelop my aching cock in the wet heat of his mouth. *Fuck yes!* I arch into his touch. My cock is swollen and veiny as Blake's tongue swirls over the weeping slit, gathering the pre-come oozing there.

I throw my head back and let out a deep moan as I clutch at the fur rug, fingers intertwined with the soft fabric. His meaty fingers trail over the inside of my thigh. The waves of sensations coursing through my body make me want to do nothing but close my eyes and let go. I watch Blake's every breath and every movement of his lips as they slide down my rigid flesh. I reach down to rake my fingers lightly through his thick, black, wavy hair, zeroing in on that lip ring that glints in the firelight. Fuck, Blake's mouth was made to take cock. His pink lips are slick with spit; his green eyes are dark with desire. His teeth graze the head of my cock, and stars burst across my vision. "I'm gonna come, baby!"

I'm panting so hard, gripping onto the tattoos on Blake's forearm. *God, he's so sexy.* I want to drown in him. Blake looks up at me, his lips curling into a knowing smile around my cock stuffing his mouth. His voice hums low, sending a shiver through my whole body. My balls tighten, drawing up so tight I'm sure they're going to burst. He yanks off my cock, and I want to scream. *Bastard!*

"Not yet, baby." Blake pulls away and walks towards one of the dressers near the table to pull out some lube and a condom, which must have been there since high school. "Do your parents really never come here?"

I'm too busy trying to laser him with my eyes to hear his question. Blake laughs at my angry expression and kneels between my legs again. He nuzzles into my thigh, sighing deep in his throat before kissing my skin. The dark brown hairs on my thigh bristles.

Blake kisses a wet trail up my body again, creeping as his soft lips skate over my skin. I'm gasping with every move he makes and struck speechless by the time he's hovering his lips right above mine. I can't seem to get enough air of my own, and it feels like I have to steal his too as it rushes past his lips.

He dips his head down for another fiery kiss, even biting at my lower lip, and I whimper into his mouth at the delicious feeling of his teeth on my skin. Seconds later, he pulls away to replace his lips with his index finger, running it slowly over my bottom lip. A moan escapes me, and I draw his finger into my mouth with a sucking pull. The salty-sweet taste of his skin dances on my tongue. The rug shifts as he sits up, prying my knees further apart. "You're gorgeous, Kieran. Remember when I used to fuck you in my jersey? Fuck, I'm so hard thinking about it now."

He slides his index finger from my mouth and trails it down my body to the pristine skin of my ass. I groan as his fingers skirt the edges of my heated opening before slipping in. Blake leans down, hovering over me, his eyes captivated as they watch every expression on my face. With his free hand, he squirts lube onto my cock. The fat globs slide down the tip and shaft, before dripping into my crack.

Blake pumps his fingers in and out, nice and slow. My throat goes dry, lips parted as I try to breathe around the blockage in my throat. Memories of our first time assault me, and I ignore the burning sensation in my eyes as Blake takes me again after five years.

His eyes slam shut, and he takes in a sharp breath as he slides his fingers in, slowly at first, until his eyes finally flutter open again and I'm staring into the storm playing out within them.

"Fuck, Blake," I rasp, my heart caving in.

The pulling and flexing of every muscle in his arm is captivating as he continues to work me open. His dark eyes don't break from mine as he leans down and whispers against my lips. "I got you, baby," he mutters and then curls his fingers.

He hits that bundle of nerves so swiftly I cry out. My back bows hard. "Blake!"

"I'm gonna fuck you," Blake says, his voice thick with lust, and slides his hand to my hip as he withdraws his fingers. I whine at the loss and barely have time to adjust before the head of this thick cock is pushing at my entrance.

A low, heavy moan pushes past Blake's lips as he pushes in. I cry out, scrambling to grab his arms for purchase as he thrusts his cock in. He isn't small by any means. His thick cock pulses, and I grunt when I feel him bottom out, the hairs over his crotch brushing against my taut ass. "Fuck, Kieran!"

Blake snaps his hips forward, and my brain turns into mush. I grunt and moan, leaning up to graze my teeth over the sensitive skin on Blake's neck, sucking on his thick Adam's apple. His hands are warm against my sides as his cock plunges deep within me, adding to the sensations that are threatening to overtake me. It's all becoming too much, but I can't let go. I can't let myself fall over that exquisite edge. "*Fuck!*" Blake's cock plunges so deep, a spangled ray of fireworks erupts over my eyes. My entire body shudders and it takes everything not to come there and then.

I bite at my lower lip, nearly breaking the skin. Soft lips brush over my skin as he whispers against my ear. It's dizzying, maddening. It's so easy to get lost in his breathy words and his hushed tone. Another intense wave of sensations washes over me, like waves of the ocean crashing over the shoreline.

*I can't fight it any longer. I can't hold on.*

"Blake—I'm gonna come—fuck, I'm coming!"

Everything I had been holding back, holding onto, vanishes with those words. The chains holding me break, and the entire world ceases to be. All I know is Blake's lips hovering above mine, his breath sweeping over my skin, the taste of his mouth, and the way he feels around me.

Everything blurs, pulses. *Fuck.*

An explosion of bright white streaks dance across my vision. My own breathing, harsh and roaring in my ears, is the only evidence there's any air left in my lungs. The heat. *Oh, God, the heat.* It seems to radiate from my core, and just when I think I might burn alive, I'm hit with an intense chill as all my muscles tense. Somewhere in the corners of my mind, I can hear Blake's charged voice and feel his lips whispering against my overheated skin as the release shudders through every part of my body.

"Fuck, baby—I'm coming!" Blake's hips snap uncontrollably, fucking me through the most intense orgasm I've ever had in my entire life. His cock twitches in my asshole, pumping like mad into the condom. A part of me wants to tear it off, to feel his searing come fill my tight hole once again.

My stomach clenches at the memory. Blake collapses onto my chest, his muscled back flexing as he pants to catch his breath. His blunt nails dig into my shoulder, and he pushes back slightly, straightening up and forcing himself deeper into my already gaping hole.

"Fuck, Kieran," he groans, his cock still twitching and pumping. "I'm coming again, baby—"

The rise and fall of his chest, his ragged breath escaping him in short bursts through slightly parted lips, his fluid movements. It's enough to make me dizzy all over again. His teeth graze over my collarbone, while his low, guttural groans fill my ear, and I feel every muscle in his body tense as he hurries to pull out and tear off the condom, just as his cock erupts and warmth spills over my stomach.

I suck in a shaky breath as Blake collapses into my arms, and I can feel his heart still pounding in his chest as he lies on top of me, sated and slick with sweat. I trail my fingers up and down his spine as the shivers work through his body. That was amazing. Too amazing.

Blake looks at me and thumbs my cheek. I'm too boneless to move, but my eyes widen when his thumb comes away wet. He chuckles, low and deep. "You always cry when I fuck you so deep. I missed that. I missed you."

I can't speak. There's a noose around my neck. I came here with the sole purpose of making him pay for what he did to me. Now I feel like I'm the one that's been played. I swallow around the thick knot in my throat and turn my face away, but the tears won't stop. They keep coming.

Blake. *Why did you have to destroy me?* I want to beg, but I don't. My lips are clamped shut.

"You okay?" Blake asks, then presses a kiss to my cheek.

"Fine," I force a laugh. "Damn, I'm wetter than Wild Water Kingdom."

Blake chuckles richly. "Yeah, and boy do I love it."

\*\*\*

I WAKE UP, MY MOUTH tasting like cotton and regret. I squint against the harsh sunlight filtering in. Blake's rhythmic breathing and the warmth of his body remind me of the night before, and the memories of the reunion rush back. *Did that really happen? Did I really succumb to my impulses and end up on the rug with my ex-boyfriend after five years?* Ugh, I feel like the embodiment of bad decisions. Just as I'm about to mentally berate myself further, Blake stirs, pulling me into his embrace, his grin playful and his voice laced with morning sensuality.

"How did you sleep?" he asks, his gaze fixed on mine.

"Like a brick." I want to quip, but I swallow the retort, suddenly feeling a tad self-conscious beside him. I turn to face him, looking up at Blake's rugged charm. Tribal tattoos ripple across his powerful biceps, the glint of his lip ring catches the sunlight, and his piercing green eyes make my heart skip a beat.

"Hungry?" I venture, doing my best to resist the urge to attack his mouth once more.

Blake shrugs, a mischievous gleam in his eyes. "Waffles?"

I burst into laughter. "Waffie Waffles!"

In perfect unison, we echo the silly joke from our youth. It was a dumb phrase we coined back then—a fallback plan for when hunger struck, and cooking ideas were scarce. "Waffie Waffles" would leave us in fits of laughter, a reminder of simpler times. *Oh, how I long for those uncomplicated moments.* Fuck, those were the best times. Tears sting my eyes and I have to pull away from him. I look around for my shirt and wipe off the dry come there. Blake seems content to stretch out on the rug, his long limbs splayed like a delicious snack. I gather my clothes and hurry to walk away, afraid I'll be tempted to eat him again.

I slip into a pair of loose sweatpants and set about preparing breakfast. A thin blanket of snow covers the ground outside, casting a tranquil scene. My focus turns to making those cherished "Waffie Waffles," whisking ingredients together, and losing myself in the simple act of baking.

However, before I can fully immerse myself, Blake's arms envelop me from behind, his warm breath tickling my neck. My own body is lean and fit, with a narrow waist and well-defined abs, but next to

Blake's imposing figure, I feel almost delicate. His muscular frame is like an impenetrable wall, solid and unyielding. As his lips brush against the nape of my neck, a soft sigh escapes me.

"Smells good, baby," he murmurs, and time seems to stand still.

My heart hammers, and I freeze. "Baby." That word, laden with memories, hits me like a ton of bricks. My throat constricts around the knot of emotions, and I step away abruptly. *He doesn't have the right to call me that anymore. Not after the hurt he inflicted.* The air is thick with unsaid words as our gazes lock, and in that charged moment, I realize that some wounds never truly heal.

I'm not the type to complain. Blake knows that. Even after my brother died and my parents abandoned me, I never even called them to ask why. It's the same thing with Blake. After he humiliated me in the locker rooms, I deleted him from all my social media accounts and never spoke to him again.

Avoidance. It's how I dealt with the worst types of pain.

With a strained chuckle, I attempt to recapture the lightness that we had earlier.

"Let's sit down and enjoy these," I suggest, hoping to dispel the tension that has settled between us. Blake stands there, seemingly at a loss for where to place his hands.

"Yeah, sure. Let's eat," he finally replies, his voice lacking its earlier fervor. The easy camaraderie we once shared now feels like a distant memory, and I struggle to understand where to go next. We haven't spoken in years, not since he broke my heart and I disappeared.

Blake lives in Detroit, and I live in LA. We're different people now.

I serve up the waffles. My movements are mechanical rather than enthusiastic. Operation: Un-Closet the Closet still occupies my thoughts, but I have to guard against the flood of emotions that Blake's unexpected return has triggered. He broke up with me without a second thought, and then his absence for five years felt like an unspoken rejection.

Amidst the clinking of utensils and the soft rustling of fabric, Blake's voice cuts through the silence. "Ugh, my parents want me to visit now that I'm in town," he admits with a touch of vulnerability. "I'm planning to visit them later today. Would you...consider coming?"

I mull over his invitation, weighing the past against the present, before responding with a nonchalant shrug. "Why not? I'm only here for a few days, anyway. Then I'll be heading back to LA."

"Right." A subtle twitch in Blake's brow hints at his surprise. "For your pet food tasting job?" he inquires, his tone curious yet guarded.

My eyes narrow. "How did you even find out about that?"

He gives me a deadpan look. "Facebook."

*What?* I almost spit out my waffles. "What do you mean, Facebook?" I don't have him on Facebook. In fact, I remember deleting him and blocking him on Facebook! "You've been keeping tabs on me through social media?"

A light flush spread to Blake's cheeks and he clears his throat. "I may have created a fake account and added you."

I'm not sure how I feel about that. My ex-boyfriend, who I assumed had forgotten all about me, was making fake Facebook accounts to stalk me. Huh. "Oh."

My emotions are a tangled mess. Blake's revelation about keeping tabs on me through social media, the reminder of how he shattered my heart, and now his attempt at explaining his actions—it's all too much to process. My skepticism is palpable as I fix him with a narrowed gaze. "Why?"

His gaze drops to his plate. "You wouldn't talk to me back then... how could I face you after that? God, Kieran," he trails off, frustration mingling with remorse. "I panicked when you came to hug me. The scouts were nearby, and my dad... I wasn't ready to come out, but that didn't mean that—" He stumbles over his words, a hint of desperation in his voice. "That I didn't love you. Or that—"

"Save it," I cut him off. "It doesn't mean anything." It's a lie—a thin veil over the whirlwind of feelings threatening to consume me. I push my chair back, the distance between us suddenly feeling insufficient. I need to get out of here. "I'm a bit sticky, so I'll clean up first."

My heart is racing, my mind struggling to keep up with the flood of memories and emotions that Blake's confession has triggered. I hadn't anticipated diving into this painful past so quickly.

I feel my hands tremble as I gather my plate and toss whatever I didn't eat into the compost. *Fuck. I can't stop shaking.* Blake's eyes drill a hole in the back of my neck, but I can't stay here a second longer. *I love you. Then why didn't you fight for me?* My eyes burn again. *Who cares about all that now? Who cares if I had loved him like no one else? Who cares if he was my best friend, the one person I trusted wholeheartedly?* It's all in the past. We're living separate lives, in different states. He's in Detroit, and I'm in L.A. The distance between us is more than just physical.

"*Kieran*—" Blake stands.

"I'm fine," I mutter, attempting to sound casual, to brush off the turmoil that's raging inside me. "Let's just move on." I stand at the sink, intent on washing the dishes, the simplest task to distract myself. But Blake follows, his footsteps echoing in the tense silence. He grabs my hand, his touch firm.

"You don't seem fine, Kieran."

I clench my jaw, my emotions coiled like a spring ready to snap. I can't contain my anger much longer, and the resentment I've carried for five years is surging forward.

*Not here. Not now. I can't let him see me break.*

"See any good movies lately?" I deflect, my tone laced with bitterness. "I like the new Fast and Furious. Although they really could have replaced Vin Diesel's part with a walking stick, and I'm sure the acting would have been better, too."

"Kieran." Blake's voice is soft, laced with genuine apology. "I'm sorry." His words hit me like a wave, a rush of pent-up rage and frustration. Five years of simmering resentment boil over, and suddenly, I'm consumed by a blinding fury. Sorry. That's all he has to offer after the way he humiliated me, the way he tore apart everything we had.

My grip tightens on a dish, my fingers trembling. I can't control the storm of emotions inside me. The weight of all the unresolved pain crashes over me, and without another word, I drop the dishes, the sound of shattering porcelain echoing through the room.

I can't face him any longer. I can't pretend that everything is okay when it's not. With my heart pounding, I flee the room.

# 4

## CRACKS IN THE FAÇADE

The scalding water cascades over my body, a futile attempt to wash away the turmoil that's churned within me. I stand beneath the stream, my thoughts a tempestuous swirl. Operation: Un-Closet the Closet is a failure, my grand plan unraveling faster than I could have imagined. Not that it was a slam dunk in the first place. I never wanted to actually hurt Blake, I was just so damn frustrated with how he treated me back then.

*Fuck.* I slam my fist against the tile wall, wishing that the ground would swallow me whole. I should go back. The reunion is over. My life is in LA, not here, in fucking Willowdale, Michigan. *I hate this place and everything it's done to me.*

As steam fills the small space, the sound of the door opening catches me by surprise. Blake's presence is palpable, his warmth radiating in contrast to the cold air that sweeps in with him. His arms encircle my waist, pulling me back into a secure embrace. The tender press of his lips against my neck is a soothing balm, even as my emotions remain in disarray. "I'm sorry." His voice is soft, sincere.

Every fiber of my being screams at me to push him away, to demand answers and explanations for the pain he's caused. But I find myself surrendering to the familiarity of his touch, the way his arms encircle me, and the warmth of his lips against my skin. It's easy to get lost in the moment, to let his closeness envelop me in a cocoon.

"Blake," I breathe.

"You owe me for breaking that dish and making me clean it up. Ceramic dishes aren't cheap, you know? That's at least five dollars at Walmart."

I puff a laugh and tilt my head to give him better access to my neck, the tension within me unraveling. The weight of my anger and hurt starts to dissolve under the soft press of his lips and the tender caress of his hands. Blake's large thumbs brush against my nipples, rolling them between his thumb and forefinger. "Fuck, baby," he hisses, attacking my throat with vigor.

All I can focus on is the sensation of him, the rhythm of his breath, the pulse of his heart. I moan when he reaches down and grabs my hard cock, twisting his wrist, while his other hand works my hole open. I'm still gaping from last night and we both moan when he breaches my entrance, his hot rod spearing me open. "Kieran," Blake whines, thrusting to the hilt.

My hand braces against the tile, limbs shaking from the heat, and his hard chest presses against my back. It's hard and fast. Blake drives his cock home as he sets a brutal pace.

I cry out, my arms buckling so fast that my face is pressed against the tile wall. Fuck. Blake. My Blake. Everything is searing hot. My heart feels like it's breaking into pieces. I stand there shivering, enveloped in his arms. My mind battles with my heart. I want to be angry, to demand more from him. But there's a part of me that still yearns for what we had, for the connection that had been so deeply rooted in our shared past.

"I'm gonna come, baby!" Blake cries, latching onto my neck while his cock pulsates inside my ass. Thick, white robes of come pump out like a hose. I groan, clenching around his spent cock, relishing the feeling of him deep inside me. Blake's teeth dig deep into my skin, and he turns his wrist expertly, so fast that soon I'm thrown over the edge.

"Fuck!" I scream, coming in scorching spurts onto the bathroom tiles. Large black spots dance across my vision, and the walls fade into a blistering white haze. Blake.

*I love you.* My entire body goes boneless, but he pulls me back against his chest. It strikes me then, like a fist to the gut, that I never stopped.

***

As we stand amidst the post-shower mist, wrapped in a tangle of limbs and warmth, reality begins to seep back in when the water grows cold. Blake laughs and reaches over to turn it off. We both step out of the shower to get dressed, my body still shivering from more than the wet water.

We'll have to hit the road if we want to visit Blake's parents. Blake's collarbone is a canvas of phantom kisses, his hair a wild mess that defies gravity. He glances at me, a playful grin tugging at his lips. "Well, that was quite the morning workout, huh?"

I can't help but chuckle, feeling the aftermath of our shared activities in every muscle. "Oh yeah, who needs a gym when you have... well, this?" I gesture between us, and we both dissolve into laughter.

"Fucking is always the best way to lose weight," Blake mutters.

I slip into a pair of dark jeans and a sweatshirt, my reflection in the mirror a mix of rug head and post-coital glow. As Blake rifles through my dresser, I notice some of Blake's old clothes still hanging around.

He pulls out a set of deep blue jeans with his underwear, socks, and t-shirts.

My cheeks warm, and I blurt out, "T-That was there when I got here! I promise I'm not keeping these as souvenirs."

Blake raises an eyebrow. "Sure, buddy, whatever you say," he teases, slipping into a black button-up shirt that makes his muscles bulge. "I'm surprised these still fit."

I reach for a bit of hair gel, attempting to tame my unruly locks. Meanwhile, Blake lets his hair flop over his forehead like he's auditioning for a shampoo commercial. "You know, you're really channeling that 'just woke up like this' vibe," I joke, unable to suppress my grin.

He gives me a mock-offended look. "Hey, effortless rug head is an art form."

I can't help but laugh at that. It's like we're picking up where we left off, a well-worn comedy routine with a dash of romance. And it's messing with my head. Shouldn't I hate him? Want to kill him and hide his body in a ditch in my backyard? Why do I feel like he feels the same? Not the killing part, but the other stuff. *Fuck*. After getting dressed, we set out, the cold air nipping at our cheeks as I slip into my trusty winter coat. We approach Blake's sleek white Mercedes Benz.

"Ah, the chariot awaits, my prince."

"Shut up and get in before I leave you here."

As we drive off, I glance at him with a grin. "You know, if anyone told me five years ago that I'd be riding shotgun in your fancy car, I would've thought they were drunk."

He chuckles, his hand finding mine on the center console. "If anyone would be drunk, it would be you. Probably hallucinating on the sidewalk."

I bark a laugh, shaking my head.

"Well, stranger things have happened." Blake's voice sounds wistful, and his warm hand fits perfectly in my own. Falling back into this routine seems dangerous, but I can't help myself. I've always wanted him and no time between us could ever make me stop.

\*\*\*

WE CRUISE INTO THE suburban jungle, where Christmas lights and decorations wage a friendly war for the title of "Most Extravagant Display." Blake parks the car in front of a house that's been transformed into a glowing beacon of festive cheer. Seriously, I half-expect Santa to pop out any minute with a "Ho ho ho!"

Stepping out, a gust of chilly air slaps me awake, making me question the idea of leaving my cozy cocoon. The abode, in contrast, practically emanates warmth, like a snug oven on Thanksgiving. Blake unlocks the door before making his grand entrance. "Mom, Dad, I'm home!" he hollers for his parents like he's about to unveil a surprise on a talk show.

Sheron descends the staircase holding a wine glass like it's the Holy Grail. "Blake, darling." Her voice drips with elegance. And then she spots me. "Kieran, you little minx!"

"Not little," I say back before I'm embraced in a hug that rivals a professional wrestler's bear hug. Ah, Sheron, the hugger extraordinaire. Her glossy black hair mirrors Blake's, but her eyes are like warm emeralds, setting her apart from the family resemblance. It's like stepping into a time machine that takes me back to the days when life was simple and hugs were the answer to everything. "It's been years since you've come back here! And so cute too!" She pinches my cheek.

"What took you so long? Blake has been a moping mess ever since you left for UCLA. Why didn't you boys tell me you were in—"

"Mom," Blake cuts in, clearing his throat.

Sheron gives him a knowing look and doesn't continue that line of thought. In what? It almost sounds like she was going to say 'in love', which certainly couldn't be the case. Blake wasn't out to his parents, right?

Then the house trembles, not from an earthquake, but from the approach of Blake's dad, Nathaniel. I half-expect the floor to crack beneath him like he's the Hulk.

"Blake? Is that you?" His voice echoes through the entire house, even to the farthest corners — okay, slight exaggeration, but he's a man of grandeur, towering at 6'6. Even Blake, who's got muscles to spare, looks like a twig next to him.

"I'm here, Dad!"

Nathaniel's hearty laugh, however, seems to have its own gravitational pull.

After some sincere hugs and firm slaps on the back, Nathaniel spots me like he's just found a hidden Easter egg. "Kieran, damn, boy, it's been too long." He claps me on the back, the force nearly knocking me into one of his vintage cars displays. "How've you been?"

"I've been good, Mr. Bryan. Hey, do you still sneak into your basement at night just to whisper sweet nothings to your vintage cars?"

"Of course, I do," he sputters, affronted that I would think he'd ever stop doing it. "Come and have a look; let the woman do the cooking."

"I heard that!" Sheron sneers. "And don't think I won't throw your ridiculous car painting set in the trash can!"

Nathaniel laughs as he ushers me toward the lower level, where his prized collection rests. "Your threats mean nothing!" He leans in closer to me. "She's been saying that for ten years. After the first five, it lost its edge."

"I'll bet," I chuckle as we go down the steps. Cars have always been the tie that binds us beyond time and distance. Nathaniel and I had a strange love for all things vintage, and I couldn't wait to see what he'd done with the models over the years. We get started, and Nathaniel finds my old stool he gave me in grade school. I can't help but sigh as I pick up a car as if no time has passed. "So, I heard Blake made it to the NHL?" I venture, taking a seat in the designated chair as we study the chaotic yet mesmerizing paint job on a 1989 Corvette.

Nathaniel lets out a weary sigh, his tone carrying the weight of a thousand parental concerns. "I honestly don't know what that boy is thinking."

"What do you mean?"

"He dropped out of UCLA after only one semester before returning to Michigan."

My ears must have been clogged because I didn't understand a thing Nathaniel was saying. "Huh?"

"Blake said he didn't belong there...besides you and him were having your lovers spat so he came back."

My hand falters mid-air, nearly dropping the delicate vintage car I'd been inspecting. "What? Didn't the Los Angeles Kings sign Blake?"

"Yes, he should've gone to UCLA like we had planned. But at the last minute, he decided to join the Detroit Red Wings." He shakes his head, his disapproval clear.

I feel like I've just been hit by a double-decker bus. "But... UCLA?"

The words escape my lips in a daze. I knew Blake had a way of surprising me, but this is a curveball that's left me flabbergasted.

Nathaniel's eyes narrow, confusion etching across his features. "Didn't he tell you? He said he went there to be with you."

*Be with me? What?* Is Blake out to his parents? Impossible. He's a homophobic asshole. This doesn't make sense. The world grinds to a screeching halt. I can practically feel my heart thudding against my ribcage as if it's trying to escape the chaos within me. *Did I hear him right? Los Angeles Kings? UCLA? Blake had been at the same university as me, and he never mentioned it?*

The pressure in my chest builds, and the sting of unshed tears threatens my composure. I swallow the lump in my throat, struggling to find words. *Why didn't he tell me? Why keep something this big a secret?*

"Now, let me catch you up on my recent colonoscopy..." Nathaniel changes the subject, but I'm numb to the world around me, the sound of Nathaniel's voice fading into the background as my thoughts race in circles. Blake's apology, his unexpected presence, and now this revelation—it's all too much to digest. "So, they take a long tube and—"

"I have to go to the bathroom!" I almost shout, racing out of the room like my ass is on fire. I hurry to the front porch and call Rachel, hoping against hope that she's available.

"Queen bitch," Rachel says upon answering her phone.

"Rach—fuck it's me—"

"I know it's you, caller ID, doofus. You owe me a big apology for ditching me last night. In fact, you should be on your knees begging for my forgiveness—"

"Rach! I'm in a situation!"

She pauses, and then her voice turns serious. "What is it? What happened? Did Blake hurt you? Well, he can say hello to the Nutcracker—"

*Thank you so much for that visual.* "No, I just—he got into UCLA and never told me. He went there for a semester, Rach and I..." Tears sting my eyes. "Why didn't he tell me?"

There's silence on the other end, and I feel like I'm missing something. "Rach..." Then it dawns on me. How badly she pushed for me to go to the reunion, and how it seemed almost like she knew this would happen. "Did you—did you know about it?"

"Yeah. I knew."

My heart slams against my ribcage. She knew the whole time my ex-boyfriend and the love of my life went to UCLA and didn't say anything to me. "*Rach, what the fuck—*"

"He asked me not to say anything. What did you expect me to do? You blocked him on everything. Anytime I brought up his name, it was like you had a shield deflector. You avoided anything to do with him."

"I—he called me a fucking fag in front of his friends—"

"I know. And he's a bastard for doing that, but, Kieran, did you ever wait for him to explain why he did that? Or what led up to that day?"

"No. Have you?" I bark, my anger rising. There are no excuses for homophobia. I didn't care how deeply in the closet he was or how much he justified it. Her silence tells me everything I need to know, and betrayal shoots right through me. "Rach—"

"Listen to him, Kieran. Sometimes people make mistakes. Back then you were out and proud, but Blake...things were different with him."

I can't believe what I'm hearing. It's almost as if she's saying that I made the mistake. That I should have waited instead of jumping to conclusions and leaving shortly after that game. My chest cracks out and tears slip down my cheeks. "What are you saying? Are you saying I made the mistake?"

"Oh, honey, I'm not saying that, but the type of love you have with Blake only comes once in a lifetime. You have a second chance at it. Why not see where it leads, okay?"

Sobs wrack my chest. Everything is coming crumbling down. I can't trust Blake not to hurt me again. I know if he does, this time it will be worse. *God, I hate her. I hate her so much*. I cup my mouth, trying to stifle my cries of anguish.

"Where are you? I'll come get you."

"Don't. I'm..." I say through tears. "I'm with Blake. With his parents... God, Rach, it's like no time has gone by. Like he's still mine."

Rachel pauses. "Maybe he always was."

I let the words sink into my soul, grounding me. Blake had been so apologetic since we saw each other again and I knew that he meant it. He was truly sorry for what happened back then between us. There's some noise in the background and I can hear Rachel's family screaming at the TV. Rachel whispers something to someone before coming back on the line. "Are you sure you're okay? You can come here. There's plenty of room."

"I'm fine," I say, taking a stuttering breath. I dry my eyes and stare off into the twinkling lights. "You should get back to your family."

"Okay, honey. I love you. Just give him a chance. You might be surprised by what happens when you do."

"Alright, I love you too."

"Okay! Call me later!" We both end the call and I'm left standing outside, the cold biting at my skin. The Christmas lights twinkle around me, their cheerful glow a stark contrast to the turmoil inside me. Blake's sudden return has turned my world upside down, and I'm left grappling with emotions I thought were buried deep in the past. The night sky is a canvas of stars, and I release a heavy sigh, the plumes of breath mingling with the winter air. *Did Blake come back for me? Did he try to find me after I disappeared from his online world?* Our history replays in my mind—our unspoken feelings, the bitter words, and the silence that followed. Half of it was my fault.

*Coming out was a big deal.* For most men, it was hard. My parents just never cared. How could I expect the same for Blake? Why are things so complicated? Why can't we just be together and figure out the rest later? I wanted to know Blake's reasons for treating me like that, but a part of me feared his response. *God, getting back together with Blake was like a plot twist in a soap opera I didn't sign up for. Just when I thought I had the script of my life figured out, they threw in a cliffhanger.*

A warm hand envelops my waist, and Blake's scruffy beard brushes against my cheek. "Ready to eat? You and Dad were having quite the chat." His voice holds a mix of playfulness and uncertainty.

I stand there, trying to gather my nerves, and Blake presses harder against me when I don't respond. "Are you okay? Did something happen? Your face is all flushed."

"I...I'm..."

I turn to face him, my eyes reflecting a storm of emotions. There's so much I want to ask, so much I want to say. But as I look into Blake's eyes, all the words I've rehearsed evaporate into thin air.

"Baby, what's wrong?" Blake asks, his green eyes searching my face. His tousled black hair falls effortlessly over his brow while his lips, a delicate shade of pale pink, are pulled into a tight line. And then there it is—the lip ring—a silver glint against his skin. There are no words for how much I love him.

Instead of answering, I press a soft kiss on his cheek, letting my actions speak for the jumbled mess of emotions within me. "I'm fine."

"Okay. Good, let's eat and then take a walk around the Christmas market later."

With a small nod, I follow him back inside the house, where dinner has come to a close, and the air is filled with warmth and laughter. We stay for another hour or so before we bid Sheron and Nathaniel farewell, promising to return soon. I find myself beside Blake once again inside his car. His hand finds mine, fingers intertwining in a gesture that's both familiar and new. With a quick smile and a shared understanding, he steers the sleek white Mercedes out of the driveway, and we drive through the night. This feels real. Right. Rachel's words replay in my head as he drives onward.

*Maybe he always was.*

Yes. Maybe.

# 5

## FORGED IN FLAMES

N avigating through the city's labyrinth of lights, we finally find a parking spot that feels like a holiday miracle. The Christmas lights cast a vibrant, almost surreal glow on the streets, and the air is infused with the smell of roasted chestnuts and festive joy. People of all ages stroll past us, bundled up in coats, their cheeks flushed with the cold and excitement.

With a wicked grin, Blake points out a display that looks like Christmas threw up all over it. I can't help but double over in laughter. "Seriously, who designs this stuff? It's like they challenged themselves to use every Christmas cliché in one decoration."

Blake chuckles, shaking his head. "I bet they have a secret competition to see who can create the most eye-searingly festive nightmare."

We continue our merry march through the market, and Blake's arm brushes mine in a casual yet comforting way. The lights seem to dance around us, and the spirit of the season permeates the air. "You know, I heard those monstrosities are a huge hit with the neighborhood squirrels. They've started using them as meeting spots for their holiday parties."

"That explains the suspiciously elaborate nut-stuffed snowmen."

"You're a sick fuck, you know that?" Blake says, walking backward just to watch me.

"I'll take that as a compliment." I smile at him.

"Hey, want to get a drink? Alley's pub is around the corner. I think there might be a game tonight, Boston Bruins and the Montreal Canadiens."

"Count me in!" I say, my eyes lighting up. "Montreal Canadiens are gonna kick your team's ass!"

"Bruins all the way, baby!" Blake exclaims. "We've got a dynasty, my friend."

"Yeah, yeah, dynasty. But the Canadiens have a history that's older than your granny's dentures. Maurice Richard was a legend before legends were cool."

Blake scoffs. "Old school doesn't win games today. We've got Bergeron, a guy so smooth on the ice he's practically a Zamboni."

"Yeah, right? Carey Price is a wall in front of the net. And Brendan Gallagher? He's like a squirrel on espresso, relentless and everywhere." I smirk, launching my counterattack.

Blake raises an eyebrow. "Squirrels, really?"

"Hey, they're tenacious."

Blake leans in, grinning devilishly. "Tell me, Kieran, are you secretly in love with the Canadiens' red and blue?"

I laugh. "They do have a certain je ne sais quoi."

"Oh là là, it's the uniform, isn't it? Just so you know, I wouldn't mind fucking you in that." Blake pretends to swoon.

"You wish," I shot back, "At least it's not a bear on your chest."

Blake feigns offense. "Hey, the bear is majestic and fierce!"

With the cold nipping at us, we enter Alley's pub. It's like stepping into a portal to comfort, with warm lights, a faint hum of chatter, and the undeniable smell of well-loved wood. But as soon as we enter, the illusion of coziness shatters like a snow globe dropped on a hardwood floor.

*Fuck.* A chorus of cheers erupts from a group of familiar faces, Blake's former jock buddies, huddled around a table and engrossed in a game. I freeze like a deer caught in headlights, the memories of those high school days flooding back in an instant. *Shit, It's game night. No wonder they're here.*

Blake waves back. "What are you pussies doing here? Go home! Your team is going to lose."

"Come say that to my face, Bryan!" someone yells.

"Fuck you!" another voice chimes in, gaining a chorus of laughter.

Crap. I exchange a glance with Blake, my smile faltering as a wave of unease washes over me. The memories of being ridiculed and humiliated come flooding back, and I feel like I've stepped into a time warp. It's a stark reminder that some things don't change, no matter how much time has passed. This is my worst nightmare. The moment seems to slow as Marcus charges toward us like a bull seeing red. It's like a bad dream—the kind where you're stuck in quicksand and the harder you struggle, the deeper you sink.

"Blake! Is that you?" Marcus bellows, and I can practically hear the echoes of his taunts from high school. The memories rush back like a tidal wave, reminding me of years of torment and pain caused by Marcus during high school.

Fuck, as if the day couldn't get any worse. Cue Marcus, the skyscraper of muscle with a vibrant shock of ginger-red hair that probably has its own zip code. Seriously, he's so tall he might need a ladder to tie his shoes. And those leporine bright green eyes? They're like lasers, making sure you're paying attention. If he ever loses his gym membership, he could just enter a "Best Redhead Hulk" competition. Fuck my life.

"Hey, Marcus. Long time." They clasp hands. "Fuck, you look great, buddy. Sorry, I missed you during the reunion."

"No worries, man. Shit, my mom and I have been watching all your games. That slapshot you delivered was fucking gold, bro."

"Yeah man, shit's different with all the cameras, but we played our asses off that night."

"I could tell, I could tell," Marcus nods energetically. "Why don't you come join us? Kristian and the girls will be around soon, and she's been after you like crazy, man."

Blake laughs. "Yeah, fuck. It's been years. She still with—God, what's his name?" He snaps his fingers. "That nerd with the glasses?"

"Melvin? Fuck no, they broke up, bro. I heard she had his kid or some shit, but she's happy to get out of that relationship, you know? But she's bringing her friends tonight if you know what I mean." His brows wiggle, and I feel sick.

"No shit," Blake says, looking like he wants to join, and then turns as if suddenly remembering I'm beside him. "Ah, Nah, dude, I better not. I'm catching up with an old friend tonight—"

"Kieran Hunter?" Marcus' brow climbs his forehead. "No shit, bro. It's been ages. Damn, you're still following Blake around like a fucking shadow!" His laugh is loud and way too fucking cruel.

My heart jams into my throat and all the emotions from earlier come rushing back to me. I feel small and helpless around these guys, though I know I'm not. Fuck Marcus and his meathead fucking friends. Blake looks away like the asshole jock didn't just insult me in front of him.

Fine.

"Marcus Dirk," I say leisurely. "Still working with your dad at the Squeeze and Save? Man, you must be so in touch with your inner zero, considering your IQ-level is non-existent."

Marcus' face darkens. "Kieran, time really flies. Don't tell me you're the same pansy-ass fairy you were in high school."

"The one and only," I snap back. "You're still using those lines? I thought bad comedy went out of fashion with those hideous shoes you're wearing."

"Fuck you—"

"Hey," Blake snaps, placing a firm hand on Marcus' chest. "Calm down."

"Nah, bro. Who the fuck does he think he is? Why did you ever let this fucking fairy follow you around so much in high school?"

The words hit like a punch to the gut. The same words he used to mock me with, the words that cut deeper than any physical blow. Anger boils within me, my hands balling into fists. My first instinct is to flee, to escape this nightmare. "Fuck you too," I spit and stride out.

***

I STORM OUT OF THE BAR, the frigid wind slapping against my cheeks. Blake's footsteps pound behind me, but I don't care. I'm sick of his jock friends reducing me to a punchline. The poison of hate and humiliation coils within me, making me so angry I can't see straight. My fists clench at my sides, and I fight to contain the storm inside.

"Kieran—wait—stop—"

"Don't fucking touch me!" I shove him off and keep walking. People are staring at us on the sidewalk, but I can't give a fuck. I'm so done with this place. With him.

"Kieran, he's an asshole. Don't take what he says seriously. Just calm down—"

"I won't fucking calm down. People like him are the reason we're treated so badly! And you just stood there like a Goddamn coward!" I seethe.

"What?" Blake grabs my arms and spins me around. "No, I didn't, but I'm not going to fight him in a bar—"

"It's not just that!" I throw my arms in the air, furious now. "You never fucking stood up for me or defended me against them! I was your fucking boyfriend! And you let them all think I was just your Goddamn stalker!" I'm screaming before I even register it.

"What did you expect?" Blake flings the words back in my face. "I was eighteen—I wasn't out yet and you—you forced me to come out!"

I stare at him like I'd been slapped. "*What?*"

Blake's jaw works, his eyes stony. "That day, you hugged me in the locker room. I told you before I wasn't ready to come out and you—*force it*. Force me. Like you were fucking daring me to deny you, and I—*you knew I'd panic*. Christ, you had years to come out and then you only give me a few seconds!"

"I didn't *force* you to come out, Blake, I—"

"You did, whether or not you want to accept it. You came inside the locker room and hugged me. Intimately. You knew what they'd think. What they'd say, and I fucking panicked! I'm sorry. I'm not perfect. Everything just slipped out, but you fucked up too," Blake snarls, his hands curling into fists. "You fucking left me. Blocked me on social media. Deleted me like I didn't exist. *I was so*—" His mouth slams shut. "I was so fucking in love with you, but you never gave me another chance. To explain."

I was stunned into silence. No. That's not how it went. I—we went our separate ways. That's all. Right? Nathaniel's words ring in my ear. Blake went to UCLA for an entire semester. He created fake Facebook accounts just to be near me and keep up with what I was doing with my life. Yes, Blake panicked and made a mistake, but so did I.

*Shit. I wrote him off completely without communicating with him.*

"Fuck—*Blake*—"

"And do you know the worst part?" Blake's bottom lip trembles, tears sliding down his cheeks. "It's that you never once asked me if I was out now. Or if I came out after you blocked me on social media."

*God, I'm such a fool.* All these years, I never considered how rough it would be for him. How hard things were for someone like Blake, captain of the hockey team, and having the world look at him to come out. The worst part is that I was thinking about outing him. *Fuck what the hell is wrong with me?* I take a step forward, but Blake takes a step back, his chest heaving. "Shit. I'm sorry—"

"Forget it," Blake says, his voice hard as stone. "We're all meatheads anyway, just like you said. You'll go back to LA, and I'll stay in Detroit." He reaches into his pocket, pulls out a gaudy Christmas squirrel, and throws it at my chest.

Blake must have bought it when I wasn't looking.

"Here, Merry fucking Christmas." He turns and walks away.

Blake is about to leave, walk out of my life forever, and I can't let him do that. We've wasted five years already and I will never let him go. *Not now.* He takes several steps before I run to him, wrapping my arms around his waist and hugging him, face pressed against his back, tears falling down my cheeks. "*I'm sorry. I love you. I never stopped. Please, Blake.*" I sob so hard my vision blurs.

Blake stills before turning around. He takes me into his arms, his own tears falling. "I love you too, so much, Kieran. You're my best friend. My everything. Don't leave me again."

I nod. "I won't. I swear. Please."

Then he does something I never thought he would. He claims my lips, right there and then.

*** 

I CLING TO HIM TIGHTLY, feeling like he is my only hope, and I kiss him with an uncontrollable passion. Blake's response is immediate, his mouth moving against mine in a passionate dance. A soft groan escapes him as his tongue slips into my mouth, and I feel the intensity of our connection surge through me. When we finally pull apart, our breaths are ragged, and my heart drums a wild rhythm in my chest. His touch lingers on my jaw, his eyes glistening with emotion. I gently brush away his tears, and we share a moment of wordless understanding.

Looking around, I see that the curious eyes have turned away, leaving us to ourselves. "Come on." Blake's voice is warm and inviting as he entwines our fingers. "Let's enjoy the game together." His grip is gentle, his touch reassuring, and I'm torn between staying hidden and embracing our truth. As we approach the pub, I hesitate, my worry resurfacing.

"Maybe we should avoid causing a scene," I suggest, but Blake seems determined.

"No, let's not hide anymore," he asserts. "I want to have a drink with my boyfriend."

His words send a flush of both embarrassment and pride through me. We clasp hands and step back into the pub, the jocks' noise filling the air. Marcus's voice cuts through the room, brimming with hostility. "No fairies allowed," he sneers, causing everyone to stop and stare.

My face burns with embarrassment, and I clench my fists, ready to confront Marcus, but Blake steps forward.

"No bigots either," Blake retorts, his tone unwavering. "So, unless you want everyone to know how you flunked every single class since grade school, you need to sit your ass down, before I lose my temper."

"Yeah, Marcus, didn't you hear? It's a 'Fierce Fairies and Fabulous Friends' kind of night. You're welcome to stay if you promise not to crush our sparkle."

The room erupts in laughter, and Marcus looks like he'd rather vanish into thin air. Meanwhile, the tall and handsome guy sitting nearby extends a welcoming hand to Blake. "Come sit with us," he grins. "We've got a strict 'No Judgment, All Fun' policy here. I'm Wilson Jenkins," he introduces himself with a grin, shaking my hand. "This is my boyfriend, Paul." He gestures to the man beside him, who smiles and nods in greeting. "We've known Blake for years since he came out after high school."

Shock courses through me. *Blake came out and kept it from me?* Regret tugs at my chest. I should have been there for him, should have listened when he needed me. But it's not too late.

Under the table, I grip Blake's hand, finding solace in his touch. He takes his seat behind me, his breath teasing my ear. "I'm sorry," I whisper, my voice tinged with guilt.

Blake's laughter rumbles in his chest, sending a shiver down my spine. "Don't worry," he replies, his tone light. "You have a lifetime to make it up to me."

\*\*\*

## 1 year later...

I'M KNEE-DEEP IN CARDBOARD chaos, packing away bits of my life and occasionally sighing like a melodramatic movie character. The new year has kicked in, and Blake and I are all hyped up to kick it off in none other than the thrilling town of Willowdale. I can practically hear you say, "Willowdale what?" Hold your horses, because our love story is about to put that place on the map. Love conquers everything, even questionable zip codes. So, here I am, about to dive into the wild world of being someone's better half. Me, the guy who once struggled to keep a houseplant alive. *Miracles do happen.*

Just as the shower in the next room takes its final bow, I can't help but grin like a kid who just found a stash of candy. Blake emerges, the embodiment of casual cool, rocking jeans that are having a serious disagreement with gravity, and a black t-shirt that seems to be in a tight competition with his muscles. I lean in for a kiss, because, well, who could resist?

"Hey there, you handsome handyman. Up for some box lifting?" I ask with a wink.

"You always know the right words to turn me on," Blake says, his mouth claiming mine once more before pulling away. He's hoisting the box as if it's made of feathers. We're a dynamic packing duo, a regular Bonnie and Clyde of bubble wrap. Upon opening one box, Blake pauses, his mouth dragging into a smile. "What's this? You kept these?" He pulls out pictures of us in high school. We were at the skate park and Blake was teaching me how to play. "Damn, I look like a shrimp."

"And tasted like one too," I quip, looking at the pictures over his broad shoulder. "Wow, crazy."

"Fuck yeah," Blake sighs packing away memories and cracked dishes and mugs with equal dedication.

"So, when's the parental invasion happening?" I inquire, and before I can say "bubble wrap," the doorbell rings like an overeager party guest.

"Right on time," Blake chuckles. Our visitors? None other than the parental units, Sheron and Nathaniel, armed with Christmas gifts and probably a few embarrassing stories to share. It's a good thing our love is strong – it's going to need to be if it's going to survive their classic family storytelling.

"Hey, Mom and Dad," Blake says answering the door.

Sheron and Nathaniel breeze in, exchanging hugs that are one part warmth, two parts awkwardness. I can't help but chuckle at our unique take on festivities. You'd think we're trendsetters, bringing Christmas into the new year, but really, we're just masters of delayed gratification.

"Kieran honey, thanks for having us. I brought you some food. Where can I put it?"

I take her over to the kitchen and with a flourish that deserves its own drumroll, Sheron deposits a veritable mountain of homemade goodies on the table. My eyes widen, not just at the sight of the tantalizing spread, but also at the realization that we might be eating leftovers until Valentine's Day.

"Wow, you made all of this? How?" I ask, wondering how she could smuggle an entire turkey through the airport.

Sheron laughs. "I have my ways."

*No, seriously. How did she bring this food?* It's going to be fucking with my head until I know the answer. Nathaniel greets me with a friendly slap on the back, and I brace myself for the incoming onslaught of personal information. "Good to see you, Kieran. Now, before you made your grand exit, I was in the middle of sharing the gripping saga of my colonoscopy. You see, what they do is—"

"Will you please shut up?" Sheron's interruption, sharp and unwavering, cuts through Nathaniel's impending TMI moment like a scissor through wrapping paper. "I'm too sober for this."

*I second that.*

"Let's get some drinks going, Mom," Blake offers, saving the day like a true hero. In a move that showcases his wisdom beyond his years, Blake senses the need for a strategic retreat. He gently guides his mother into the kitchen, possibly to distract her with something stronger than the fruit punch.

Once she gets inside the kitchen, Sheron gets down to business. She unveils a spread that could easily put a five-star restaurant's buffet table to shame. My stomach practically performs a joyful jig as I take in the sight – an array of savory cured meats, an alluring assortment of cheeses, sliced turkey and ham that seems to be locked in a delicious duel, a colorful garden of veggies just begging to be devoured, and the pièce de résistance: a tantalizing pool of gravy surrounding a mound of creamy mashed potatoes. It's as if a food fairy decided to grant all of our culinary wishes at once.

My taste buds are practically salivating in anticipation, and the aroma wafting from the feast is an irresistible siren song. I open my mouth to ask Sheron the inevitable question – *How on earth did she manage to sneak this feast past airport security?* – when the doorbell suddenly rings, like a plot twist we didn't see coming.

"Is that your friend? Is she coming too?" Sheron calls out.

"Yeah, Rach should be here now—" I start to explain, only to be interrupted by the entrance of none other than Rachel, gliding into the room with Miles in tow.

*What the fuck?* My jaw practically clatters to the floor, my eyes widening in a mix of disbelief and amusement. When did this little rendezvous get planned? I shoot Rachel a playful but scandalized look before pulling her into a hug and making a mental note to get the full story later. *I totally thought Miles was gay, and my gaydar is never wrong.*

Miles extends a hand, which I shake warmly, and he takes in the surroundings with a whistle. "Wow, nice digs, man."

I turn to Rachel who raises her brow at me, daring me to question why Miles is here with her. I mouth 'what the fuck' to her and she shakes her head, her long dreadlocks cascading down her back.

"I'll tell you all the filthy and juicy stuff later," Rachel purrs, and I'm scared.

"Is that a terrace?" Miles' eyes widen as he checks out my penthouse apartment. "Damn, bro. This place is crazy."

"Thanks," I reply, my chest puffing out a bit with pride before I remember the impending relocation.

Blake slides an arm around me, a silent yet strong gesture of support.

Miles raises an eyebrow, clearly intrigued. "You're leaving all this behind?"

"Yeah, that and my pet food tasting job."

Miles' brows climb. "Are you sure you aren't going to miss it?"

I share a knowing glance with Blake. "Nah, not even a little bit."

### *THE END*

— · —

# EPILOGUE

"Rach, you and Miles are so perfect together. How did you two end up together, anyway?" I ask, sipping my coffee. We're sitting in my bedroom while everyone else is in the kitchen finishing up dessert.

Rachel's eyes sparkle with mischief as she begins, "Well, it's a funny story. We both love football, and we meet up at a game a few months back. I guess he's there doing some promotional stuff, and I'm passionately cheering for my team, and he's, well, on the losing side, to put it kindly."

I can't help but laugh. "So, love blossoms on the battlefield?"

Rachel nods, grinning. "You could say that. We start talking during half-time, and he can't resist poking fun at my team's terrible defense. We just hit it off. Miles is so different in high school, I guess things change. We meet up at games, grab a coffee afterward, and chat about everything from our favorite players to our ridiculous game-day superstitions. But what seals the deal is when he gets me a jersey with his favorite player's name. Inside the jersey, there's a note asking if I'd be his date to the next game."

I chuckle. "Now, that's a clever move."

"We're inseparable ever since. Even though we still argue about our teams."

"I thought he was gay though?" I ask.

"Gay? Miles? Nah, he's just gender-fluid. Bisexual, I think. To be honest, I'm not really listening. We don't believe in labels," Rach says, pinching my arm as I laugh at her. "Come on! We're missing the party!" She drags me back into the kitchen.

## OTHER WORKS

### Blades of Desire (Book #1)

Hockey is like my personal battlefield, and it's also where I escape my everyday troubles. You see, my brother's injury is this big dark cloud that just won't go away. And guess who I've got to thank for that never-ending shadow? Grayson Hayes, the guy with the magic touch for bringing misery.

So, picture this: I've got a one-way ticket to Revengeville, and guess who's the mayor? Yep, Grayson. The hockey rink is where I plan to give him a lesson in pain, the kind he served my brother. My thirst for payback is like an itch I can't scratch, and I've been scratching that itch for ages.

But hold on to your helmets, because here's the plot twist: those lines between who's hunting and who's being hunted? They're like doodles in a kid's coloring book. And the shocker? I'm the one who's gone outside the lines. It turns out my revenge plan has turned into someone else's game board.

Hockey used to be my escape from a tough life overshadowed by my brother's serious injury. I was mad as a goalie facing a breakaway, all thanks to Grayson Hayes, the guy who put my brother in that spot. Finally, I get my chance to face Grayson, and I'm all fired up to make him sweat.

But after one hot and steamy night in the locker room, things get even more interesting. My quest for revenge takes an unexpected turn when I start feeling drawn to Grayson. I'm caught between my anger and these strange new feelings. Plus, there's a whole mystery unfolding beyond our rivalry. Can I come out on top, not just in the game, but maybe even in a wild romance with my sworn enemy?

## Cross Blades (Book #2)

Once inseparable, my best friend and I were torn apart after a night of fiery passion—a memory forever etched in my mind, its details lost in a hazy fog. Now, Alex May is my bitter rival, his indifference cutting deeper than any blade. The looming national state championships intensify the stakes, fueling the fire of that unforgettable night.

In the arena's dim light, tension crackles. Each stride, each thud of the puck, echoes unspoken words. The remnants of our once unbreakable bond intertwine with a burning desire for vindication.

I yearn to reach out to Alex, hoping he'll give me a second chance. But his walls are high, his heart guarded. Will he ever forgive me for the mistakes of our past and allow love to mend our broken connection?

## Heated Rivalry (Book #3)

With graduation looming, I'm forced to take an extra credit athletic course in hockey—a sport I despise. The ice, the cold, and the game itself are everything I detest. But when a bone-shattering shove on the ice threatens to fracture my knee, I must confront my fears and learn to play.

In a shocking revelation, I discover it was Devon who had shoved me hard on the ice.

Devon Black.

A demon. A force to be reckoned with, notorious for his bullying tactics on and off the ice.

I hate Devon with every fiber of my being, yet beneath the surface of my hatred lies an undeniable and confusing attraction. It's as if the very essence of him is both repulsive and magnetic, drawing me in against my will.

Graduation approaches and the choices we make will determine our fate—whether bitter separation or a love that transcends the icy battleground we call home. Can Devon and I bridge the divide, or will life's forces tear us apart?

— · —

# Author's Note

J.M. Jackie is a writer who specializes in crafting dark and twisted novels, exploring complex human relationships and the darker side of love and desire. She enjoys drinking black coffee and taking long walks with her two large dogs for inspiration. While her writing can be intense, she aims to create stories that challenge readers to confront their own assumptions and beliefs while providing an escape into a richly imagined world of adventure, magic, and occasionally martial arts!